**For childhood best friends everywhere,
but especially for G.E.M.**

**"Friendship is the golden thread
that ties the heart of all the world."
——John Evelyn**

Library of Congress Cataloging-in-Publication Data
Names: Graegin, Stephanie, author.
Title: The long ride home / Stephanie Graegin.
Description: First edition. | New York : Random House Studio, [2022] | Audience: Ages 4–8 | Summary: "A story that
celebrates memories and friendship about a young koala and a friend who has moved away" —Provided by publisher.
Identifiers: LCCN 2021042528 (print) | LCCN 2021042529 (ebook) | ISBN 978-0-593-42602-9 (hardcover)
ISBN 978-0-593-42603-6 (lib. bdg.) | ISBN 978-0-593-42604-3 (ebook)
Subjects: CYAC: Memory—Fiction. | Friendship—Fiction.
Classification: LCC PZ7.1.G713 Lo 2022 (print) | LCC PZ7.1.G713 (ebook) | DDC [E]—dc23

The artwork in this book was drawn in Adobe Fresco and colored in Adobe Photoshop.
The text of this book is set in 16.5-point Belle MT Pro Semibold.
Interior design by Rachael Cole

MANUFACTURED IN CHINA
10 9 8 7 6 5 4 3 2 1
First Edition

the long ride home

stephanie graegin

RANDOM HOUSE STUDIO
NEW YORK

On the long ride home,
so much makes me think of you.

The music shop reminds me of when I met you.

You were playing a kazoo
and I knew right away
we would be best friends.

There's the ice cream parlor
we would go to.

I'd get mint chip and you, strawberry cream—
you'd tell me stories and I would tell you stories too.
We had uncontrollable giggles.
No one makes me laugh like you do.

When we pass the big hill,
I close my eyes and I can remember us there.

Remember that day we rode our bikes too close?
The worst part was that I had to go home early.

I still have a scar on my knee.
But that's okay because it reminds me of you.

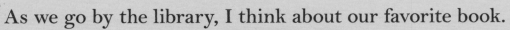
As we go by the library, I think about our favorite book.

You know, the one with the green cover.

I still borrow it again and again.

I will never get tired of it.

Will you?

We went to a party
at the yellow house once.

It was loud and I didn't like it.
You stayed by me,
even though you wanted to dance.

Today the breeze feels like a gentle, warm hug—
like standing by the sea.

It reminds me of my favorite day.
We drove drove drove
with your mama to the beach
and sang songs all the way.

Then we floated all afternoon, just you and me.
We talked for hours about all sorts of stuff,
but when we were quiet that was nice too.
I can still smell the coconut sunblock.

We got to stay up past our bedtime.

Do you remember the way the moon looked?

I think about that day a lot.

Even cardboard makes
me think of you!

You understand why I get excited
about an empty box.

Maybe when we are grown up
we can live in houses side by side.

You understand a lot of things about me.

There's your old house.
But you're not there.

I wonder what you are doing right now.

I wonder if you are thinking about me.